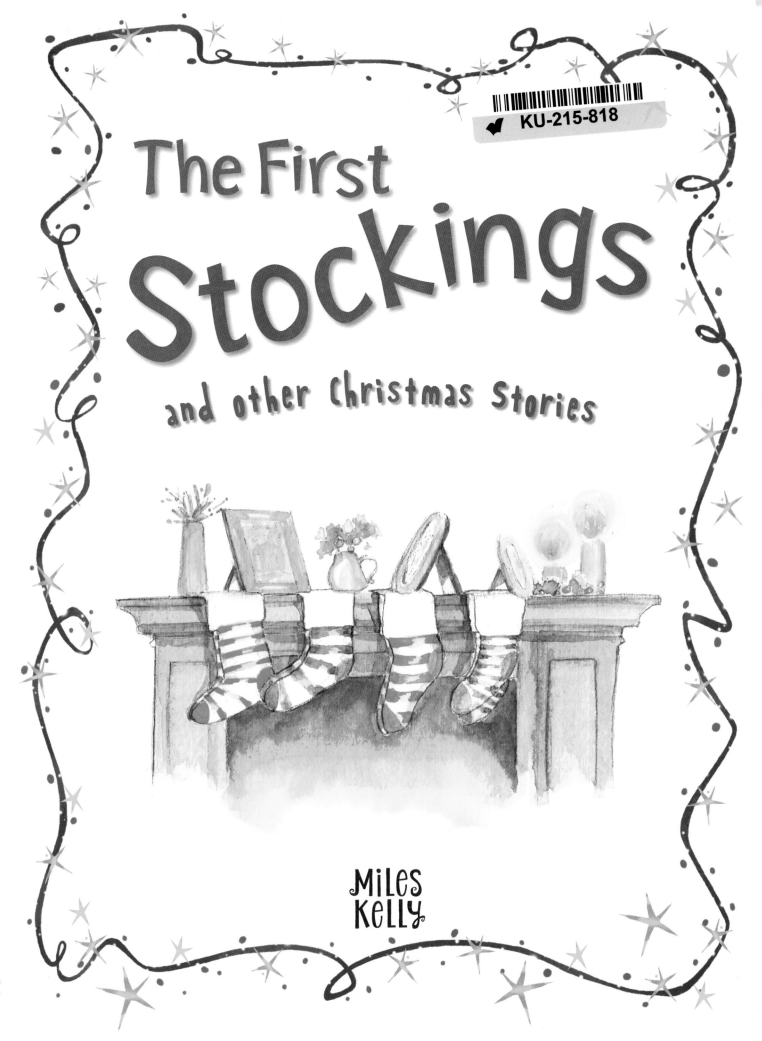

The First Stockings

and other Christmas Stories

MILES KELLY

First published in 2015 by Miles Kelly Publishing Ltd
Harding's Barn, Bardfield End Green, Thaxted, Essex, CM6 3PX, UK

This edition printed 2018

2 4 6 8 10 9 7 5 3

Publishing Director Belinda Gallagher
Creative Director Jo Cowan
Editorial Director Rosie Neave
Senior Editor Sarah Parkin
Design Manager Joe Jones
Production Elizabeth Collins, Jennifer Brunwin-Jones
Reprographics Stephan Davis, Jennifer Cozens, Thom Allaway
Assets Lorraine King

ISBN 978-1-78209-826-3

Printed in China

British Library Cataloguing-in-Publication Data
A catalogue record for this book is available from the British Library

ACKNOWLEDGEMENTS
The publishers would like to thank the following artists who have contributed to this book:

Front cover: Simona Sanfilippo (Plum Pudding Illustration Agency)

Inside illustrations:
Decorative frame Rachel Cloyne (Pickled Ink)
The Little Match Girl Simona Sanfilippo (Plum Pudding Illustration Agency)
The First Stockings Florencia Denis (Plum Pudding Illustration Agency)
Little Women's Christmas Breakfast Charlotte Cooke (The Bright Agency)
Aunt Cyrilla's Christmas Basket Natalia Moore (Advocate Art)

Made with paper from a sustainable forest

www.mileskelly.net

Contents

The Little Match Girl

Adapted from a story by
Hans Christian Andersen

It was dreadfully cold. It was snowing fast and was almost dark as evening came on.

In the cold and the darkness went a poor little girl, walking slowly along the street barefoot. When she left home she had shoes on, but they were much too big for her feet and the poor little girl lost them in running across the street.

So on the little girl went with her bare feet that were blue with cold. In an old

apron that she wore were bundles of matches, which she sold to passersby to make a few pennies each day, and she carried a bundle also in her hand. No one had bought so much as a bunch all day, and no one had given her even a penny.

Poor little girl! Shivering with cold and hunger she crept along, a picture of misery.

The snowflakes fell on her long blonde hair, which hung down in curls. Lights gleamed in every window, and there came to her the delicious smell of roast goose, for it was New Year's Eve.

In a corner, she sat down shivering. She drew her little feet under her, but still

she grew colder and colder. She did not dare go home until she had sold some matches. And, besides, it was cold enough at home, for they had only the roof above them, and though the largest holes had been blocked with straw and rags, there were many holes left through which the cold wind whistled.

Her little hands were nearly frozen with cold. She couldn't help thinking a single match might do her good if she might only draw it from the bundle, rub it against the wall, and warm her fingers by it. So at last she drew one out and struck it. *Fzzzzit!* It blazed and burned! It gave out a warm, bright flame like a little candle, as she held one hand and then another over it.

A wonderful little light it was. It really seemed to the little girl as if she sat before a great iron stove with polished brass feet.

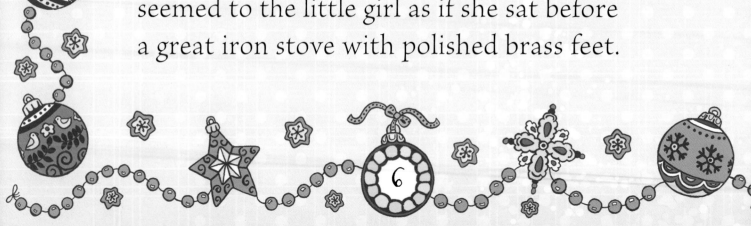

The little girl stretched out her feet to warm them also. How comfortable she was! But then the flame went out, the stove vanished, and nothing remained but the little burnt match in her hand.

She rubbed another match against the wall. It burned brightly, and where the light fell upon the wall it became transparent like a veil, so that she could see through it into the room. A clean white cloth was spread upon the table, on which was a beautiful china dinner service. A roast goose, stuffed with apples lay upon a platter, sending up wisps of steam and smelling delicious. And then what was still more wonderful, the goose jumped from the dish and waddled along the floor straight to the little girl.

But then the little match went out, and nothing was left but the thick, damp wall.

She lit another match. And now she was under a most beautiful Christmas tree, larger and far more pretty than the one she had seen through the glass doors at the rich merchant's. Hundreds of wax candles were burning on the green branches, and bright baubles twinkled down upon her. The child stretched out her hands to them, then the match went out.

Still the lights of the Christmas tree rose higher and higher. She saw them now as stars in heaven, and one of them fell, forming a long trail of fire.

"Now someone is

dying," murmured the little girl softly, for her grandmother, the only person who had loved her, who was now dead, had told her that when a star falls a soul flies up to God.

She struck yet another match against the wall, and again it was light. And in the brightness there appeared before her the little girl's dear old grandmother, bright and radiant, yet kind and sweet, and happy as she had never looked on earth.

"Oh, Grandmother," cried the child, "take me with you. I know you will go away when the match burns out. You, too, will vanish, like the warm stove, the splendid New Year's feast, the beautiful Christmas tree." And in terror that her grandmother should disappear, she rubbed the whole bundle of matches against the wall.

And the matches burned with such a brilliant light that it became brighter than midday. Her grandmother had never looked so beautiful. She took the little girl in her arms, and both flew together, joyously and gloriously, far above the Earth. And for them there was neither hunger, nor cold, nor care – they were with God.

But in the corner, at the dawn of day, sat the little girl, stiff and cold, with the matches, one bundle of which was burned.

"She wanted to warm herself," people said. No one imagined what wonderful visions she had had, or how gloriously she had gone with her grandmother to enter upon the joys of a new year.

The First Stockings

An extract from *The Life and Adventures of Santa Claus*
by L Frank Baum

*This is part of a story telling how Santa Claus invented
the first toys and then, with the help of his reindeers Flossie
and Glossie, took them to children's houses.*

When you remember that no child,
until Santa Claus began his travels,
had ever known the pleasure of possessing a
toy, you will understand how joy crept into
the homes of those who had been favoured
with a visit from the good man.

When another Christmas Eve drew near there was a load of beautiful gifts for the children ready to be loaded upon the big sledge. Claus filled three sacks, and tucked every corner of the sledge full of toys.

Then, at twilight, the ten reindeer appeared and Flossie introduced them all to Claus. They were Racer and Pacer, Reckless and Speckless, Fearless and Peerless, and Ready and Steady, who, with Glossie and Flossie, made up the ten who have traversed the world these hundreds of years with their generous master. They were all very beautiful, with slender limbs, spreading antlers, velvety dark eyes and smooth coats of fawn colour spotted with white. Claus loved them at once, and has loved them ever since.

The new harness fitted them nicely and soon they were all fastened to the sledge by twos, with Glossie and Flossie in the lead. The reindeer wore strings of sleigh bells, and were so delighted with the music they made that they kept prancing up and down to make the bells ring.

Claus seated himself in the sledge, drew a warm robe over his knees and his fur cap over his ears, and cracked his whip as a signal to start.

The reindeer leapt forwards and were

13

away just like the wind, while jolly Santa
Claus laughed gleefully to see them run, and
shouted a song in his big, hearty voice:

With a ho, ho, ho!
And a ha, ha, ha!
And a ho, ho, ha, ha, hee!
Now away we go
O'er the frozen snow,
As merry as we can be!
There are many joys
In our load of toys,
As many a child will know;
We'll scatter them wide
On our wild night ride
O'er the crisp and sparkling snow!

Now it was on this Christmas Eve that
little Margot and her brother Dick, and her
cousins Ned and Sara, who were visiting
at Margot's house, came in from making

a snowman. The children's clothes were damp, their mittens dripping, and their shoes and stockings wet through. They were not scolded, for Margot's mother knew the snow was melting, but they were sent to bed early so that their clothes might be hung over chairs to dry.

The children's shoes were placed on the red tiles of the hearth, where the heat from the hot embers would strike them, and their stockings were carefully hung in a row by the chimney, directly over the fireplace.

That was the reason Santa Claus noticed them when he came down the chimney that night, once the household was fast asleep. He was in a tremendous hurry, and seeing the stockings all belonged to children, he quickly stuffed his toys into them and dashed up the chimney again, appearing on

the roof so suddenly that the reindeer were astonished.

'I wish they would all hang up their stockings,' he thought, as he drove to the next chimney. 'It would save me a lot of time and I could then visit more children before daybreak.'

When Margot and Dick and Ned and Sara jumped out of bed the next morning and ran downstairs to get their stockings from the fireplace, they were filled with delight to find the toys from Santa Claus inside them. In fact, I think they found more presents in their stockings than any other children of that city had received, for Santa Claus was in a hurry and did not stop to count the toys.

The First Stockings

The children told all their little friends about it, and of course every one of them decided to hang their own stockings by the fireplace the next Christmas Eve.

On his next trip Santa Claus found so many stockings hung up in anticipation of his visit that he could fill them in a jiffy. He could be away again in half the time required to find the children and place the toys by their bedsides.

The custom grew year after year, and has always been a great help to Santa Claus.

Little Women's Christmas Breakfast

An extract from *Little Women*
by Louisa May Alcott

*Jo, Meg, Amy and Beth have been told their mother
can't afford any Christmas presents this year, apart from one
dollar each and a book. They've decided to buy presents for their
mother with their money – handkerchiefs, slippers, gloves and
a bottle of cologne. Their father is away at war.*

Jo was the first to wake in the grey dawn of Christmas morning. No stockings hung at the fireplace, and for a moment she felt disappointed. Then she remembered

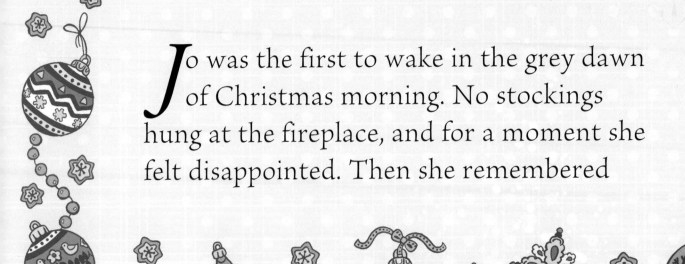

her mother's promise and, slipping her hand under her pillow, drew out a little crimson-covered book. She woke Meg with a 'Merry Christmas' and bade her see what was under her pillow. A green-covered book appeared. Presently Beth and Amy woke to rummage and find their little books also, one dove-coloured, the other blue, and all sat looking at and talking about them, while the east grew rosy with the coming day.

"I'm glad mine is blue," said Amy, and then the rooms were very still while the pages were softly turned, and the winter sunshine crept in to touch the bright heads with a Christmas greeting.

"Where is Mother?" asked Meg, as she and Jo ran down to thank her for their gifts, half an hour later.

"Goodness only knows. Some poor

person came a-beggin', and your ma went straight off to see what was needed. There never was such a woman for givin' away," replied Hannah, who had lived with the family since Meg was born, and was considered by them all more as a friend than a servant.

"She will be back soon, I think, so have everything ready," said Meg, looking over the presents, which were collected in a basket and kept under the sofa, ready to be produced at the proper time. "Why, where is Amy's bottle of cologne?" she added, as the little flask did not appear.

"She took it out a minute ago and went off with it to put a ribbon on it, or some such notion," replied Jo, while she danced about the room.

"How nice my handkerchiefs look, don't

they? Hannah washed and ironed them for me, but I marked them all myself," said Beth, looking proudly at the somewhat uneven letters that had cost her such labour.

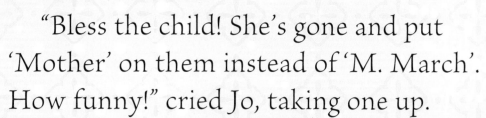

"Bless the child! She's gone and put 'Mother' on them instead of 'M. March'. How funny!" cried Jo, taking one up.

"Isn't that right? I thought it was better to do it so, because Meg's initials are M.M., and I don't want anyone to use these but Marmee," said Beth, looking troubled.

"It's all right, dear, and a very pretty idea. Quite sensible too, for no one can ever mistake them now. It will please her very much, I know," said Meg, with a frown for Jo and a smile for Beth.

"There's Mother. Hide the basket, quick!" cried Jo, as a door slammed and steps sounded in the hall.

Amy came in hastily, and saw her sisters all waiting for her.

"Where have you been, and what are you hiding behind you?" asked Meg.

"Don't laugh at me, Jo! I didn't think anyone should know till the time came. I only meant to change the little bottle of cologne for a big one, and I gave all my money to get it."

As she spoke, Amy showed the handsome flask that replaced the cheap one, and looked so earnest that Meg hugged her on the spot, while Beth ran to the window and picked her finest rose to ornament the stately bottle.

Another bang of the street door sent the

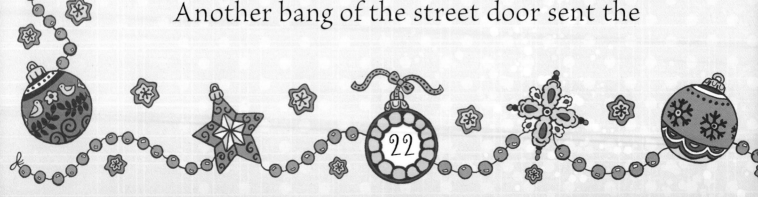

basket under the sofa, and the girls to the table, eager for breakfast.

"Merry Christmas, Marmee! Many of them! Thank you for our books," they all cried in chorus.

"Merry Christmas, little daughters. I want to say one word before we sit down. Not far away from here lies a poor woman with a little newborn baby. Six children are huddled into one bed to keep from freezing, for they have no fire. There is nothing to eat over there, and the oldest boy came to tell me they were suffering hunger and cold. My girls, will you give them your breakfast as a Christmas present?"

They were all hungry, having waited nearly an hour, and for a minute no one spoke, but only a minute, for Jo exclaimed, "I'm so glad you came before we began!"

"May I go and help carry the things to the poor little children?" asked Beth eagerly.

"I shall take the cream and the muffins," added Amy, heroically giving up the article she most liked.

Meg was covering the buckwheats, and piling the bread onto one big plate.

"I thought you'd do it," said Mrs March, smiling as if satisfied. "You shall all come and help me, and when we come back we will have bread and milk for breakfast, and make it up at dinnertime."

They were soon ready, and the little procession set out.

A poor, bare, miserable room it was, with broken windows, no fire, ragged bedclothes, a sick mother, a wailing baby, and a group of pale, hungry children huddled under one old quilt, trying to keep warm.

How the big eyes stared and the blue lips smiled as the girls went in.

"It is good angels come to us!" said the poor woman, crying for joy.

"Funny angels in hoods and mittens," said Jo, and set them to laughing.

In a few minutes it really did seem as if kind spirits had been at work there. Hannah, who had carried wood, made a fire, and stopped up the broken window panes. Mrs March gave the mother tea and gruel, and comforted her with promises of help, while she dressed the little baby as tenderly as if it had been her own. The girls set the food on the table, sat the children round the fire, and fed them like so many hungry birds, laughing, talking, and trying to understand the funny broken English.

That was a very happy breakfast, though

they didn't get any of it. And when they went away, leaving comfort behind, I think there were not in all the city four merrier people than the hungry little girls who gave away their breakfasts, and contented themselves with only bread and milk on Christmas morning.

"That's loving our neighbour better than ourselves, and I like it," said Meg.

The girls set out their presents while their mother was upstairs collecting clothes for the poor family.

Not a very splendid show, but there was a great deal of love done up in the few little bundles, and the tall vase of red roses, white chrysanthemums and trailing vines, which stood in the middle, gave quite an elegant air to the table.

"She's coming! Strike up, Beth! Open

the door, Amy! Three cheers for Marmee!"
cried Jo, prancing about while Meg went to
conduct Mother to the seat of honour.

Mrs March was both surprised and
touched, and smiled as she examined her
presents and read the little notes that
accompanied them.

The slippers went on at once, a new
handkerchief was slipped into her pocket,
scented with Amy's cologne, the rose was
fastened in her bosom, and the nice gloves
were pronounced a perfect fit.

Aunt Cyrilla's Christmas Basket

Adapted from a story
by L M Montgomery

When Lucy Rose met Aunt Cyrilla coming downstairs with a big, flat-covered basket hanging over her arm, she gave a little sigh.

"Aunt Cyrilla," she said, "you're surely not going to take that funny old basket to Pembroke – Christmas Day and all."

"I'm not a mite worried about its looks," returned Aunt Cyrilla calmly. "If it hurts your feelings to walk with a countrified old

29

lady with a basket, you can just fall behind."
She nodded and smiled good-humouredly.

"Now, let me see," said Aunt Cyrilla,
"what shall I take? That big fruit cake
and those three mince pies. That plate of
jelly cookies and doughnuts will please
the children, and that ice-cream
candy and the striped candy
sticks. And apples, of
course, two pots of
my greengage
preserves. And
sandwiches and
pound cake for
a snack. The
presents for the
children can go
in on top. There's
a doll for Daisy and

the little boat for Ray. Now, is that all?"

"There's a cold roast chicken in the pantry," said Lucy Rose wickedly.

Aunt Cyrilla smiled broadly. "Since you have reminded me of it, the chicken may as well go in."

Lucy Rose, in spite of her prejudices, helped with the packing and did it very well too. But when Aunt Cyrilla tied the bulging covers down, Lucy Rose stood over the basket and whispered, "Someday I'm going to burn this basket. Then there'll be an end of lugging it everywhere we go."

Uncle Leopold came in just then, shaking his head. "I doubt you folks'll get to Pembroke tomorrow," he said sagely. "It's going to storm."

Next morning Uncle Leopold drove Aunt Cyrilla and Lucy Rose and the basket

to the station, though the air was thick with flying flakes.

When their train came along Aunt Cyrilla looked beamingly around her at her fellow travellers. These were few in number – a delicate little woman with a baby and four other children, a young girl with a pale, pretty face, a sunburnt lad in a khaki uniform, a very handsome old lady in a sealskin coat ahead of him, and a thin young man with spectacles opposite.

"A minister," reflected Aunt Cyrilla, "and that woman in the sealskin is cross at something, and that young chap must be not long out of the hospital."

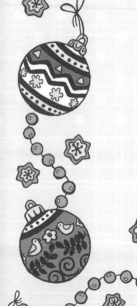

They expected to reach Pembroke that night, but as the day wore on the storm grew worse. Twice the train had to stop while the train hands dug it out. The third time it could not go on. It was dusk when the conductor came through the train.

"Impossible to go on or back – track blocked for miles. I'm afraid we're here for the night."

"Oh, dear," groaned Lucy Rose.

Aunt Cyrilla looked at her basket. "At any rate, we won't starve," she said.

The sealskin lady looked crosser than ever. The khaki boy said, "Just my luck," and two of the children began to cry. Aunt Cyrilla took some apples and striped candy sticks from her basket. She lifted the oldest into her ample lap and soon had them all around her, laughing and contented.

The rest of the travellers straggled over to the corner and drifted into conversation. The khaki boy said it was hard lines not to get home for Christmas, after all.

"I reached Halifax three days ago and telegraphed the old folks I'd eat my Christmas dinner with them. They'll be so disappointed." He looked very disappointed too. Aunt Cyrilla passed him an apple.

"We were all going down to Grandpa's for Christmas," said the little mother's oldest boy. "We've never been there before, and it's just too bad."

The pale, pretty girl came up and took the baby from the tired mother. "What a dear little fellow," she said softly.

"Are you going home for Christmas too?" asked Aunt Cyrilla.

The girl shook her head. "I'm just a shop girl out of work at present, and I'm going to Pembroke to look for some."

Aunt Cyrilla went to her basket and took out her box of ice-cream candy. "I guess we might as well enjoy ourselves. Let's have a good time."

The little group grew cheerful as they nibbled, and even the sealskin lady brightened up.

By and by the children fell asleep. Aunt Cyrilla and the pale girl helped the mother make up beds for them.

"We must get up some Santa Claus stuff for these youngsters," said the khaki boy. "Let's hang their stockings on the wall and fill them up as best we can. I've nothing but some cash and a knife. I'll give each of them a quarter and the boy can have the knife."

"I've nothing but money either," said the sealskin lady.

Aunt Cyrilla glanced at the little mother. She had fallen asleep.

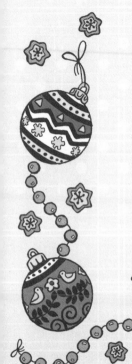

"I've got a basket over there," said Aunt Cyrilla firmly, "and I've some presents in it. I'm going to give them to these. As for the money, I think the mother is the one for it to go to. Let's make up a little purse among us for a Christmas present."

The khaki boy passed his cap and everybody contributed. The sealskin lady put in a note for twenty dollars.

Meanwhile, Lucy Rose had brought the basket. She smiled at Aunt Cyrilla as she lugged it down the aisle, and Aunt Cyrilla smiled back. Lucy Rose had never touched that basket of her own accord before.

Ray's boat went to Jacky, and Daisy's doll to his oldest sister. Then the stockings were filled up with doughnuts and jelly cookies, and the money was put in an envelope and pinned to the mother's jacket.

When morning came the storm was still raging. The children wakened and went wild with delight over their stockings. The little mother found her envelope and tried to utter her thanks. Then the conductor came in and told them they'd be spending

Christmas on the train. Aunt Cyrilla rose
to the occasion.

"I've got some
emergency rations
here," she announced.
"There's plenty for
all and we'll have our
Christmas dinner,
although a cold one.
Breakfast first thing.
There's a sandwich
apiece left, and what
is left of the cookies
and doughnuts."

At noon they had
dinner. The train hands
were invited in to share it.
The minister carved the chicken
with the brakeman's knife, and the khaki

boy cut up the mince pies. Bits of paper served as plates. Everybody declared they had never enjoyed a meal more in their lives. The bones of 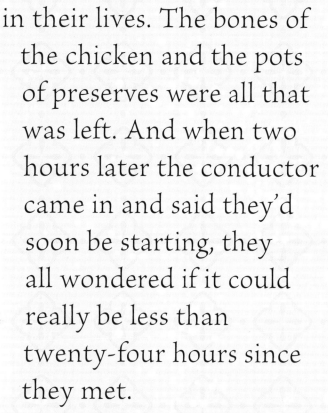 the chicken and the pots of preserves were all that was left. And when two hours later the conductor came in and said they'd soon be starting, they all wondered if it could really be less than twenty-four hours since they met.

At the next station they all parted. The little mother and the children had to take the next train back home. The minister stayed there, and the khaki boy

and the sealskin lady changed trains. The sealskin lady shook Aunt Cyrilla's hand. She no longer looked cross.

"This has been the pleasantest Christmas I have ever spent," she said. "I shall never forget your wonderful basket. The little shop girl is going home with me, and I've promised her a place in my husband's store."

When Aunt Cyrilla and Lucy Rose reached Pembroke there was nobody there to meet them, so they elected to walk.

"I'll carry the basket," said Lucy Rose. "It's a blessed old basket and I love it. Please forget all the silly things I ever said about it, Aunt Cyrilla."